JIGSAW JACKSON

JIGSAW JACKSON

BY

DAVID F. BIRCHMAN

ILLUSTRATED BY

DANIEL SAN SOUCI

LOTHROP, LEE & SHEPARD BOOKS   NEW YORK

J. JACKSON
21 French Fry Ln.

To my brother Fred, artiste extraordinaire
—DFB

To my brother Robert, auteur extraordinaire
—DS

Text copyright © 1996 by David F. Birchman
Illustrations copyright © 1996 by Daniel San Souci
All rights reserved. No part of this book may be reproduced or utilized in any form or by any means,
electronic or mechanical, including photocopying and recording, or by any information storage and retrieval system,
without permission in writing from the Publisher. Inquiries should be addressed to
Lothrop, Lee & Shepard Books, a division of William Morrow & Company, Inc., 1350 Avenue of the Americas,
New York, New York 10019.
Printed in the United States of America
First Edition   1 2 3 4 5 6 7 8 9 10
Library of Congress Cataloging in Publication Data
Birchman, David Francis. Jigsaw Jackson / by David F. Birchman; illustrated by Daniel San Souci.
p.   cm.   Summary: J. Jupiter Jackson, a potato farmer, discovers he is a genius at jigsaw puzzles,
and so one winter he leaves the farm and his animals to seek fame and fortune.
ISBN 0-688-11632-9. — ISBN 0-688-11633-7 (lib. bdg.)
[1. Jigsaw puzzles—Fiction. 2. Farm life—Fiction. 3. Domestic animals—Fiction.] I. San Souci, Daniel, ill.
II. Title. PZ7.B511877Ji   1996   [E]—dc20   94-48815
CIP AC

The illustrations in this book were done in watercolor paints. The display type was set in Decorated 035 BT.
The text was set in Schneidler. Color separations prepared by Colotone Graphics.
Printed and bound by Worzalla Publishing Company. Production supervision by Linda Palladino.

WAY UP IN SAPONAC, MAINE, there once lived a young potato farmer named J. Jupiter Jackson. Now potato farming is hard work most of the year, but come winter—after the potatoes have been dug up and bagged, the blue winds are howling, and snow is filling the world right up to the barn eaves—then there just isn't a whole lot to do.

J. Jupiter did his best to keep busy. He played checkers with the plow horse, read stories to the chickens and the barn mice, and listened to opera recordings with his pet mynah bird.

He also fixed things. Folks brought him their broken clocks, busted harrows, beat-up buggy wheels, and battered bed boards. The trouble was, J. Jupiter Jackson had such a knack for putting things back together that the work took him no time at all—and no time at all isn't much time when you're trying to fill up a long winter.

No doubt J. J. Jackson would have let the years pass on without raising a fuss about the long cold winters, but fate can be fickle, even for young potato farmers. Late one November day, a stranger driving a wagon loaded high with small cardboard boxes came up the road to J. Jupiter Jackson's farm. The wagon stopped in front of the farmhouse, and the driver hopped down and reached out to shake J. Jupiter Jackson's hand.

"Greetings, Mr. Jackson," he said. "I'm Sean Shane O'Riley McShaker, the world's greatest jigsaw-puzzle maker, and I bet you're the kind of fellow who could use one of my puzzles. There's nothing like puzzling to fill up the long gray winter."

"What's a jigsaw puzzle?" asked J. Jupiter Jackson.

"You've never seen a jigsaw puzzle?" exclaimed Sean McShaker. "Well, let me show you one!" He pulled the farmer into the house, sat him down, and dumped the contents of a box onto the table. "These are puzzle pieces," he said, picking up a piece in each hand. "The trick is to find the pieces that fit together."

"You mean like this?" said Jackson. He reached into the pile, picked out two pieces, and joined them together. They fit perfectly.

Sean McShaker nodded and smiled. "That's it. You've already got the hang of it. Now you just keep fitting the pieces together until there are none left. I sell these puzzles for a dollar a box. I'd say two boxes ought to see you through the winter. That will be two dollars cash."

"I don't think two boxes will do," sighed J. Jupiter Jackson.

McShaker looked down at the table. His jaw dropped below the knot of his tie. The puzzle was all put together, whole and complete. "Say, Mr. Jackson, could you do that for me again?" He dumped out the contents of a bigger puzzle box. In less than a blink, J. Jupiter had put it all together.

"How do you do that?" asked Sean McShaker.

"I just join the pieces that fit together, and I don't join the pieces that don't fit together," said J. Jupiter.

"Mister, you're a puzzling phenom!" exclaimed Sean McShaker. "You've just got to go on the road with me. What a team! The world's greatest jigsaw-puzzle maker and the world's greatest jigsaw-puzzle joiner. Why, I can hear it now—*Ladies and gentlemen, introducing J. J. Jackson, the jigsaw champ-een. Nobody, but nobody, can unjumble and join the jigs in a jigsaw faster than "Jigsaw" Jackson!* We'll be famous."

J. Jupiter Jackson considered the proposal. He didn't like the idea of leaving his animals alone, but then he thought about the howling blue winds, the snow filling the world up to the barn eaves, and the long days with nothing to do. "Well, I guess it wouldn't hurt to leave the farm for a little while," he finally said, "provided I can get back before potato-planting time."

The next morning he said good-bye to the animals, climbed onto Sean McShaker's puzzle wagon, and they headed down the eastern seaboard.

In every town they passed through, Sean McShaker challenged all comers to a jigsaw puzzle contest—the winner being the first to complete a five-hundred-piece jigsaw puzzle. At first Jigsaw Jackson faced his opponents one-on-one. Then McShaker began to challenge ten, twenty, thirty, forty, and fifty people at one time. The harder the challenge, the faster Jigsaw Jackson got, and the more puzzles Sean McShaker sold.

By early January the two men had reached New York City.

"Plain old jigsaw puzzles aren't good enough for these folks," said Sean McShaker knowingly. "These folks are sophisticated. If you want to impress these folks, you have to do something special."

As they rounded the corner they came smack-dab on an enormous circus poster plastered against a nine-foot-high wooden fence. The poster, filled with all kinds of hoopla, read:

COME ONE, COME ALL
TO BISON BOB'S
WILD WEST EXTRAVAGANZA!!!

"That's it!" cried Sean McShaker. "There's our something special. I'm going to take my jigsaw machine and jigsaw this circus poster into a thousand pieces. Then we're going to pay Bison Bob a visit."

And that's how, for the first and only time in recorded history, a jigsaw-puzzle joiner became a Wild West circus star. At the start of each show, Bison Bob came charging into the big top riding two bison abreast, and Jigsaw Jackson commenced to assemble the enormous poster puzzle in the center ring. The crowd thrilled to the sound of thundering hooves and the slapping together of puzzle pieces. Bison Bob did back flips as the puzzle pieces whirled through the air. By the time Bison Bob had circled the center ring three times, Jigsaw had the entire nine-foot poster done and complete.

Jigsaw Jackson became an overnight celebrity. Letters and telegraph messages poured in from everywhere. Most were congratulatory, but one was not:

```
DEAR J. JUPITER JACKSON— STOP—

WHEN ARE YOU COMING HOME?— STOP—

THE CHICKENS AND THE BARN MICE MISS

   THEIR STORIES— STOP—

YOURS SINCERELY, THE PLOW HORSE— STOP.
```

"Don't mind that old plug," said Sean McShaker. "The circus was okay for starters, but now it's time to do something really extra-special. And I have just that extra-special something in mind."

That night McShaker broke into the New York Museum of Very Expensive Art with his jigsaw machine and jigsawed up all the very expensive pictures. The next morning, museum-goers didn't have to walk from gallery to gallery to look at the pictures—they were all jigsawed up into a single stupendous pile. Everybody was shocked and horrified until Sean McShaker stepped out from behind the pile with Jigsaw Jackson. "Ladies and gentlemen," he roared, "this here is J. J. Jackson, the jigsaw champ-een. Nobody, but nobody, can unjumble and join the jigs in a jigsaw faster than Jigsaw Jackson! So just stand back and give this man some elbow space."

Jigsaw rolled up his sleeves and went straight to work. His hands and arms became one large swirl of color. Flying puzzle pieces filled the air like autumn in an egg beater. By the end of the day, not only had he joined all the pictures back together without a seam to be seen, but he had put them back into their gold frames and hung them back on the walls.

"Jigsaw Jackson" became a household word. Mothers held their babies up to him in the street to be kissed. He received telephone calls from all over the country. Most were calls of acclamation, but one was not. "Mr. Jackson," said the small, shrill voice on the other end of the line, "it's the mynah bird. Please come home, Mr. Jackson. The plow horse misses his checkers."

"Don't pay any mind to that birdbrain," said Sean McShaker. "Now it's time for something really extra-extra-special. And I have just the extra-extra-special something in mind that will put you in the history books for sure."

That night Sean McShaker went down to the pond in Central Park with his jigsaw machine, jigsawed out all the ice, and piled it up on the north shore.

The next morning Jigsaw Jackson put the gigantic ice puzzle together in front of a crowd of chilled but eager spectators. He started off slowly to get the hang of joining the ice. Then he gradually built up his speed. Soon he was moving along like a one-man blizzard. He only stopped now and again to clean off his goggles and break the icicles off his nose—still the work took one whole day. That night all the pieces of the puzzle froze together into a single slab, so Sean McShaker rounded up several dozen taxicabs and had them push the sheet of ice back over the pond.

The gigantic ice puzzle brought Jigsaw Jackson worldwide recognition. All kinds of people dropped by to visit. Most of the visitors came to applaud and show their profound admiration, but one group did not.

"You've just got to come home, Mr. Jackson," pleaded the chickens and the barn mice. "The mynah bird misses his opera records something awful."

Just as Jigsaw Jackson opened his mouth to reply, Sean McShaker came running up the stairs waving a letter. "It's from the president!" he shouted. "The president wants you to display your jigsaw-joining talent before the United States Congress. Both houses!"

"Well, I don't know," said Jigsaw. "Maybe I ought to be getting back to the farm."

McShaker's face suddenly turned red. "You've been listening to those clucks and squeaks, haven't you? It's time you forgot about that potato farm of yours. You're big potatoes now," he said. Then he stepped between Jigsaw Jackson and his visitors and slammed the door.

After the Wild West circus, the art museum, and the ice pond, Jigsaw's performance before the United States Congress seemed like child's play. All he had to do was put together a jigsawed, wall-sized picture of General George Washington crossing the Delaware. There were no more than ten thousand puzzle pieces, and the task took him no more than fifteen minutes. When he was through, the building rang with thunderous applause. Jigsaw Jackson bowed several times and began to leave. Then he noticed the president was whispering to the Senator from Maine and pointing at the picture. He turned to see what all the fuss was about. There, right in the middle of the picture, a jigsaw piece was missing!

Now everyone knows that no greater calamity can happen to a jigsaw joiner than to finish a jigsaw puzzle and discover that a piece is missing. You can imagine how Jigsaw Jackson felt when he saw that empty space right at the tip of General George Washington's nose. It was as if someone had jigsawed his heart into a hundred pieces. He knew then that his puzzle-joining days were over.

That very night, J. Jupiter Jackson caught the train for Saponac.
After all he'd been through, it was a relief to return to the potato
farm, the plow horse, the chickens, the barn mice, and the pet
mynah bird.

The rest of that winter was as long as ever, but come spring, J. J.
Jackson married a widow with nine children—nine children who
broke things faster than even he could fix them. Somehow the
winters were never so long again.

Sean McShaker continued to make and sell puzzles, but he never went back to Maine. He moved way out west to California, where he had heard the ground had a habit of trembling and jigsawing up all by itself.

There's just one piece missing from this story: What happened to that puzzle piece? It remains a mystery to this day. I suspect that there are those who know the answer—but they just aren't talking.